On Wimbledon Common, under the ground in their Burrow, live

The WOMBLES

Tomsk to the Rescue

Adapted by Elisabeth Beresford

from the Wombles television series produced by CINAR and UFTP

Hodder
Children's
Books

a division of Hodder Headline plc

Wellington had just had one of his great ideas!
He would build a Weather Station so that the
Wombles could tell what the weather was going
to be like. Wellington was going to put it in a
tree and was working down below when there
was an extraordinary noise.

"Whooooaaaaahhhhh!"

And Tomsk, hanging on to a rope, came
flying through the air. He knocked over
Wellington and sent all his bits and pieces in
all directions.

"I'm Tarzan Tomsk," said Tomsk. "What are you doing, Wellington?"

"Well, I was making a sort of Weather Station," said Wellington crossly. "I'm just going to show Tobermory how it works."

"Now I'll switch it to the wind-gauge," said Wellington.

"Hm, there seems to be quite a breeze blowing outside," Tobermory said. And then there was that extraordinary noise again . . .

"Whooooaaaaahhhhh!"

It was Tomsk showing off to Orinoco and Shansi.

"I'm Tarzan Tomsk! I swing across the jungle - well, the Common - on the jungle vines. Look, I'll show you!"

And before anyone could stop him Tomsk tried to swing across the kitchen, only he flipped over and landed on the supper table. Wallop!

"That's enough of that," said Tobermory crossly, "out you all go and do some tidying up. The wind's started to blow and there'll be rubbish everywhere!"

Tomsk went off, still pretending to himself that he was Tarzan Tomsk cleaning up the jungle.

Back in the Burrow, Madame Cholet was looking at the mess Tomsk had made of her supper table and she was not pleased at all! She gave Shansi an umbrella and asked her to go and pick some wild strawberries for supper as Tomsk had squashed the pudding when he fell on it.

The wind was getting really strong by now so Alderney and
Stepney decided to stop work and take shelter in the tree-house
until the storm was over.

But Shansi was
still out on the
Common, busy
picking strawberries.
She added one more to the pile she had tied up
in a scarf. Suddenly, she was blown clean off
her back paws and right up into the sky as she
hung on to the umbrella. Then with a thud she
landed on a top branch of the old weather tree.

"Help!" cried Shansi. "I'm up here."
"I'll rescue you," shouted Tarzan
Tomsk. And he grabbed the rope
that was still hanging from the tree.

"Whooooaaaaahhhhh!" Tomsk called, as
he swung backwards and forwards.
Up in the tree-house, Alderney and
Stepney heard all the shouting.
They tied a tablecloth to the
wheeliebarrow to make a sail, and
with the wind behind them
they rushed across the
Common to help
with the rescue.

But just as they reached the tree, there was another great gust of wind and Tomsk was blown up onto the branch where Shansi was sitting.

"Oh dear! What shall we do?"
said Shansi.
      "Hand me your umbrella," said
Tarzan Tomsk, "and hang on tight!"

And the pair of them
floated down from the
top of the tree.

Alderney and
Stepney watched
from below.

But just before the
umbrella reached the
ground, it turned inside
out and the flying
Wombles dropped down
suddenly. Shansi fell on
top of Tomsk.

"Great landing!" said Stepney.

"Oh dear, I've dropped my strawberries," said Shansi as Alderney and Stepney hurried over to them.

"Don't worry - I've got them!" said Alderney.

"Shansi?" said Tomsk.

"Yes," answered Shansi.

"Do you think I could get up now?"

They all laughed and went back to the Burrow so Madame Cholet could make her delicious strawberry shortcake for tea, while Wellington told them all about his Weather Station.